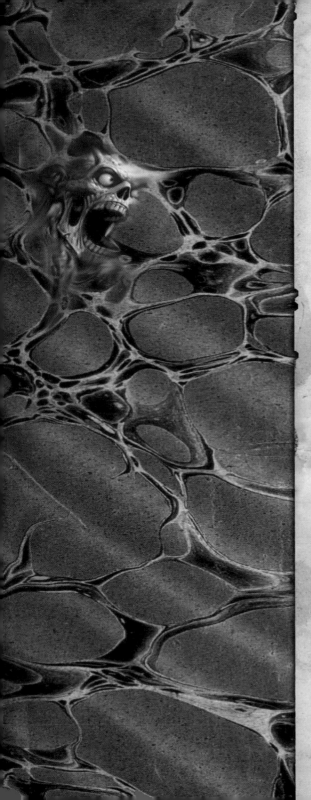

PROFESSOR JULIUS PEMBERTON-SNIDE

VAMPIRES

AND OTHER MONSTROUS CREATURES

As Carried by the Famous
Dr. Cornelius Van Helsing on His Fateful
Journey to Transylvania

Vampires and Other Monstrous Creatures

This facsimile edition has been carefully reproduced from the original volume carried by Dr. Cornelius Van Helsing on his Transylvanian journey in 1907, which was discovered by Marcus de Wolff among his father Gustav's papers in 1937.

Text and images © 2007 by HarperCollins Children's Books
Designed by Philip Chidlow for Brushfire Limited
Text by Mary-Jane Knight
Manufactured in China.

Library of Congress Cataloging-in-Publication Data is available.
ISBN 978-0-06-145412-7

1 2 3 4 5 6 7 8 9 10
First published in Great Britain in 2007 by
HarperCollins Children's Books,
a division of HarperCollins Publishers, London
First U.S. edition published 2008

Acknowledgments

Many thanks for the invaluable illustration contribution made to this project by Julian Johnson-Mortimer (www.johnson-mortimer.co.uk)

Illustration on page 76 by Paul Young (represented by Artist Partners)

VAMPIRES

AND OTHER MONSTROUS CREATURES

HarperCollins*Publishers*

CONTENTS

An Introduction to This Volume

For centuries myths and legends about Vampires have been told at firesides and hearths on dark winter nights while the wind howled outside and blew smoke down chimneys. There have been those who have sought to disprove the existence of these creatures, and yet sightings and reports of Vampires continue to appear.

This small volume attempts to offer the interested reader some carefully researched information on this popular subject. Many rare volumes have been dusted down and consulted, along with records and eyewitness accounts of sightings of Vampires and other Monstrous Creatures that strike fear and dread into the hearts of ordinary people.

As well as the most recent information on these creatures, I have included a definitive guide to identifying Vampires and those at risk of becoming a Vampire, as well as remedies from around the world for ridding ourselves of the attentions of these terrifying creatures.

—Professor Julius Pemberton-Smythe
London

PART ONE

VAMPIRES

OF THE WORLD

The Vampire: A History

The history of Vampires stretches back to ancient times. An ancient Persian vase shows a man struggling with a huge creature that is trying to suck his blood.

In ancient Babylon a deity was known to drink the blood of babies. Her name was Lilitu or Lilith, and she was reputed to be the first wife of Adam. She left her husband and became queen of the demons and evil forces.

Records of the Living Dead were found in China during the sixth century B.C. Stories and sightings of Vampires have been recorded throughout the world, including India, Malaysia, Polynesia, and the lands of the Aztecs and the Inuit. The Aztecs believed that offering the blood of young victims to the gods ensured the fertility of the earth.

But Europe is the Vampire's true home. Roman and Greek myths tell of many bloodthirsty goddesses whose names evolved into terms for witches, demons, and Vampires. During the eleventh century, both witches and doctors prescribed the blood of virgins to cure illnesses. At this time, corpses discovered intact all over Europe increased the fear of Vampires. People began to believe that those who died without receiving the last rites or those who had committed suicide or had been excommunicated were destined to return to the earth as one of the devil's minions: a Vampire or one of the Living Dead.

There are accounts of the discovery of Vampires in books such as *The Diabolical Dictionary* by the Bishop of Cahors, *The Courtiers' Triflings* by Walter Map, and *The History of England* by William of Newburgh.

An outbreak of Vampirism occurred in the fourteenth century in central Europe. The bubonic plague was believed to be the work of Vampires, and anxiety about infection led people to bury their dead without verifying that they were truly dead. Many tales of encounters with Vampires rising from their graves were recorded during this time. Not all tales were of  true Vampires. Some were unfortunates who had been buried alive and emerged covered in blood from the injuries they sustained in clawing their way out of their graves.

In the mid-fifteenth century there came the trial of Frenchman Gilles de Rais, a nobleman, soldier, and former member of Joan of Arc's guard. He was accused of torturing and murdering young children, mainly young

boys who were blond-haired and blue-eyed. He and his accomplices then set up the severed heads of the children in order to judge which was the most fair. The precise number of Rais's victims is not known, as most of the bodies were burned or buried. The number of murders was probably between eighty and two hundred. The victims ranged in age from six to eighteen and included both sexes. Although

Rais preferred boys, he would make do with young girls if circumstances required. Gilles de Rais and his accomplices were hanged for their crimes in October 1440.

The most famous historical Vampire is Vlad Tepes Dracula, Prince of Wallachia, an ancient kingdom that is now part of Romania. His double name of Tepes (meaning Impaler) and Dracula (after his father, Dracul, meaning devil or dragon) was well suited to him. He was a bloodthirsty tyrant who ordered thousands of people to be impaled (see left) for his pleasure, and it is no wonder that many suspect him of being a true Vampire. Bram Stoker's recently published novel, *Dracula*, has immortalized this evil man.

In Hungary in 1611, a female Vampire was discovered. Countess Elizabeth Bathory was accused of kidnapping and torturing young girls to death and then bathing in and drinking their blood. Her study of black magic led her to believe that this would preserve her youth and looks. When a large number of young women were reported missing, Bathory's cousin led a detachment of soldiers and policemen to capture her. She was locked up in a tower room for the rest of her life, and her accomplices were all executed.

This event in history gave rise to numerous rumors of Vampires and Vampirism. Many in southern and eastern Europe believed that werewolves (*vrykolakas* in Slavic) died and became Vampires in the hereafter. This is when

the term "Vampire" came into popular usage. It was first coined in German as Vanpir in a report of a case of Vampirism, and this evolved into Vampire in 1732.

During the eighteenth century, many set out to destroy beliefs about Vampires. Scholars, doctors, philosophers, and members of the church all cast doubt on the accomplishments of the devil and his minions. But legends of Vampires could not be stamped out. Country folk were wary of those with bushy eyebrows drawn together or hair on the palms of their hands. To detect Vampires, they employed virgins who rode black or white horses through a cemetery, knowing the horse would rear at the tomb of a Vampire. The rumor spread that those born of a union between Vampire and mortal could detect Vampires. The burial of suspected Vampires was done with special precautions, such as driving a nail into the forehead of the corpse, smearing the body with pig's fat, or placing a clove of garlic in its mouth. These were just some of the methods used to prevent the suspected Vampire from rising.

See pages 42–47 for an authoritative guide on how to detect and destroy Vampires today.

Words *for* "Vampire"
from Around *the* World

Adze – Southeastern Ghana

Algul – Arabia

Alp – Germany

Asanbosam – Ghana

Aswang – Philippines

Azeman – Surinam

Bajang – Malaysia

Bebarlangs – Philippines

Bhean Sidhe – Ireland

Bhuta – India

Bibi – Gypsy

Blutsauger – Germany

Bramaparush – India

Bruxsa – Portugal

Callicantzaro – Greece

Chordewa – Bengal

Chupacabra – Mexico

Churel/Churail – India

Civatateo – Mexico

Danag – Philippines

Dearg-due – Ireland

Dhampir – Gypsy

Doppelsauger – Germany

Empusa – Greece

Eretica – Russia

Estrie – Hebrew

Gayal – India

Ghoul – Arabic

Hannya – Japan

Impundulu – Africa

Incubus – medieval Europe

Jaracacas – Brazil

Khang-Shi/Chiang-shi – China

Kozlak – Dalmatia

Kresnik – Slovenia

Krovijac – Bulgaria

Kudlak – Slovenia

Kukutu – Albania

Lamia – Greece

Lampir – Bosnia

Langsuir – Malaysia

Leanhaum-shee – Ireland

Liderc/Ludverc – Hungary

Lobishomen – Brazil

Loogarro/Ligarro – West Indies

Lugat – Albania

Mandurago – Philippines

Mara – Scandinavia

Masan/Masani – India

Mati-anak – Malaysia

Mora – Czechoslovakia

Mormo – Greece

Moroii – Romania

Motez dam – Hebrew

Mullo/Muli – Gypsy

Muroni/Murony – Wallachia

Nachzeher – Bavaria, Silesia

Nelapsi – Slovakia

Obayifo – West Africa

Odorten – Russia

Ohyn – Poland

Penanggalan – Malaysia

Pijavica – Slovenia

Strigoii/Strigocia – Romania

Succubus – medieval Europe

Swamx – Myanmar

Tlacique – Mexico

Ubour – Bulgaria

Ulstrel – Bulgaria

Upier/Upior – Poland

Upyr/Oupyr – Russia

Vampir/Vampyr – eastern Europe

Vetala – India

Volkadlak – Slovenia

Vopyr – Russia

Vourdalak/Wurdalak – Russia

Vrykolakas – Greece

Vukodlak – Serbia

Wieszczy – Poland

Xloptuny – Russia

Zmeu – Moldavia

EUROPE

Dearg-due

Upier

Alp

Ohyn

Nachzeher

Ubour

Kudlak

Ulstrel

Nelapsi

Krovijac

Strigoii

Zmen

Lugat

Moroii

Bruxsa

Pijavica

Muroni

Dhampir

Empusa

Lamia

Civatateo

Loogarro

Azeman

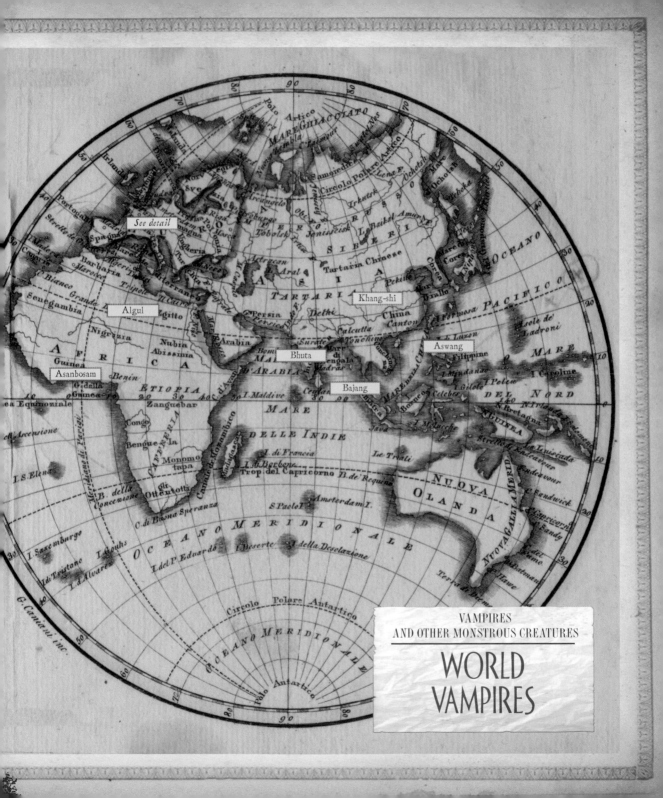

See detail

Khang-shi

Algul

Aswang

Asanbosam

Bhuta

Bajang

An A *to* Z *of* Vampires:

ALGUL An Arab Vampire whose name translates from the Arabic to mean horse-leech, bloodsucking spirit, or demon. In western countries this form of Vampire is more commonly known as a ghoul *(see page 62).*

Traditionally an algul is a female demon who feasts on dead babies and inhabits cemeteries. It may appear as half woman, half fiend. Alguls are said to devour the most recently dead bodies in a cemetery, and the sound of their chewing emanates from cemeteries at night.

The algul appears in Arabian folktales and literature, including *The Book of One Thousand and One Nights,* or *The Arabian Nights.*

Fig. 1 Alp *in* pig form

ALP This German Vampire-like spirit torments women's sleep at night. Its physical manifestations are considered highly dangerous. The alp is thought to be male and may be the spirit of a newly dead relative or a demon. If a mother uses a horse collar to ease the pain of childbirth, her child may become an alp.

It is said that an alp may appear as a cat, a pig, a bird, or a dog—perhaps even a werewolf. In all manifestations the alp wears a hat. If it loses its hat, it also loses its power, especially its invisibility and strength. As a spirit, an alp can fly like a bird and ride a horse.

An alp enters the body through the victim's mouth, via the tongue or as a mist, or it may even turn into a snake. Utter misery follows ingestion. Because it is involved in the terrors of the mind, it is virtually impossible to destroy an alp.

At night women are advised to protect themselves by sleeping with their shoes beside the bed, with the toes pointing toward the door.

Fig. 2 Algul *or* Arabian Ghoul

ASANBOSAM

This African Vampire inhabits Ghana, Ivory Coast, and Togo. The asanbosam lives in deep forests and has a generally human shape, but with iron teeth, legs with hooklike appendages, and six arms. This Vampire dangles from trees and grabs people who walk past, scooping them up and killing them. It can be male or female.

ASWANG

A Vampire of the Philippines that appears as a beautiful woman by day and a flying fiend by night. An aswang lives in a house and appears normal during the daytime. At night she visits victims' houses and sucks their blood with her long thin tongue, which she inserts through cracks in the roofs of houses.

This Vampire feeds especially on sleeping children. She can be recognized by her swollen appearance after feeding. At dawn the aswang returns to human form.

If an aswang licks someone's shadow, the person will die soon afterward. It can be repelled by garlic under the armpits.

Fig. 3 Aswang

Bats! I can never regard these creatures as anything other than a bad omen— or indeed a menace in themselves.

C

Fig. 4 Azeman

AZEMAN
A South American Vampire with the daytime form of a human female. At night she is transformed into a bat or other animal. Protections against the azeman include scattering seeds across the floor (like other Vampires, she is obsessed with counting so will stop to count them all). Also, if a broom is placed across the door, she will not enter the room, as she will count the bristles of the broom.

Fig. 5 Bajang

BAJANG
This Malaysian male demon Vampire appears often as a mewing polecat and may mew at the door of its victims. The bajang particularly threatens children. Bajangs are created by summoning the restless spirit of a stillborn child from its grave, or the transformation may be inherited as the result of the evil deeds of one's ancestors.

Fig. 6 Bruxsa

BHUTA

An Indian Vampire or malevolent spirit that is the ghost of a man who died by accident, was executed, or committed suicide. A person may also turn into a bhuta if he is not given the proper funeral rites.

Bhutas are reputed to live in cemeteries or dark, desolate places. They eat excreta or intestines. An attack by a bhuta may result in serious illness or even death, although in some cases a bhuta may simply play a trick on, or waylay, travelers.

Shrines have been built throughout India to placate the bhuta. People may protect themselves from bhutas by lying on the ground, as a bhuta would never rest on the earth. Those who worship bhutas turn into them.

Fig. 7 Ancient stone carving of a bhuta

BRUXSA

This female Vampire species originates in Portugal. She is transformed through witchcraft and flies at night in the form of a large bird. The bruxsa is known to torment travelers. She may appear in normal human form during the day, but if she has any children, she will drink their blood. There is no known way of destroying a bruxsa.

CIVATATEO

A witchlike Vampire of the Aztecs in Mexico. Noblewomen who die in childbirth return to earth in this form to wander on broomsticks, haunting temples or crossroads. They are reputed to be the servants of the Aztec god Tezcatlipoca and to have the magical powers of a priest.

Children are the civatateo's favorite victims; when attacked, they die of a wasting disease. Civatateos are shriveled and hideous, with white faces, and arms and hands covered in white chalk. Crossbones are painted on their tattered dresses or tattooed on their shrunken flesh.

Reminds me of the tales of my old Irish nurse, told by the fireside on wild winter nights—she swore on her mother's grave that her aunt had seen one of these demons. . . .

C

Fig. 8 Classical ceremonial pottery showing an empusa

DEARG-DUE
Also known as dearg-dul, this is an Irish female demon, whose name means "red blood sucker." She is believed to rise once a year from her grave and seduce men until they enter her embrace. She then sucks them dry of blood. Stones must be piled on the graves suspected of housing this beast.

DHAMPIR
In Serbia, dhampir is the child of a Vampire. The name was coined by Slavonic gypsies. If a male Vampire has a child with his widow, a dhampir results. The child can also be known as vampir (male) or vamphiera (female). Dhampirs are able to detect and destroy their Vampiric families.

EMPUSA
This vile, Vampire-like creature originated in Greek myths. Empusae are half donkey, half human but can transform themselves into beautiful maidens. In this guise they entice travelers to approach, then devour them.

KHANG-SHI
A Vampire demon from China, also known by the name chiang-shi. It is tall and has white or greenish hair over its body, long, sharp claws, terrible eyes, and fangs.

Older khang-shi can fly. They may be trapped in their graves by sprinkling them with rice, iron, and red peas. They may be destroyed by lightning.

Fig. 9 **Khang-Shi**

KROVIJAC A Bulgarian name for a Vampire (also known as vampir or ubour). This Vampire stays in its grave for four hundred days while its skeleton forms. It can be destroyed by chaining it to the grave and strewing wild roses about or by planting wild roses above the coffin.

KUDLAK A Slovenian name for a Vampire.

Fig.10 Lamia

LAMIA A lamia is a female Vampire, or Vampiric demon, who entices children to her and eats them. She may appear as a beautiful woman but have the body of a scaled lion or serpent.

Lamiae appear at night to prey on children, drinking their blood and eating their flesh. They are named after a woman in Greek legend who was the mortal lover of the god Zeus. In revenge Zeus's wife Hera made Lamia so insane that she ate all her own children. When she realized what she had done, she set out to kill the children of others.

Other traditions say that a lamia is a species of demon who has the power to remove her eyes. She entices men to their deaths, then devours them in a gruesome manner.

"The hinderparts of the beast are like unto a Goate, his fore legs like a Beares, his upper parts to a woman, the body scaled all over like a Dragon."

Anon.

LOOGARRO OR LIGARRO
A West Indian witch Vampire.

Fig. 11 Loogarro

LUGAT
An Albanian type of Vampire, also known as *kukutui*. It has similarities to other undead creatures found in the Balkans and can be hamstrung or burned to render it harmless. Other traditions describe the lugat as a formidable monster that may not be destroyed by any living thing other than a wolf, which can bite off its leg. Thus humiliated, the lugat will retire to its grave and will never be seen abroad thereafter.

MOROII
A Romanian name for a live Vampire, as opposed to a *strigoii*, which signifies a dead Vampire. A moroii may be male, in which case it is bald or balding, or it may be female and red in the face.

Fig.12 Moroii

Fig. 13 Nachzeher

MURONI (OR *MURONY*)

A Vampire from the south Romanian region of Wallachia, similar to a strigoii. It can shapeshift into almost any creature—a cat, dog, fox, flea, spider, or other animal—and stays easily in these guises. Its victims innocently believe it to be the creature it shapeshifts to resemble and are drained of blood, but they do not have puncture marks. Anyone thus slain is doomed to become a Vampire.

A muroni can be identified in its grave by its long fangs, sharp talons or claws, and the fresh blood that drips from its orifices. To destroy a muroni, you must pound a long nail through its forehead or a stake through its heart.

Fig. 14 Muroni in fox guise

NACHZEHER

An unusual German Vampire species. One may distinguish a nachzeher in its coffin by its curious custom of holding the thumb of one hand in the other hand while keeping its left eye open.

A nachzeher devours its own shroud while in the grave, then begins to feast on its own flesh. As this happens, its surviving relations begin to waste away as the life force is drawn out of their bodies. The nachzeher then leaves its coffin and visits its family, often in the guise of a pig, and drinks their blood.

Another tradition of this fearsome creature is that it may enter the belfry of a Church and ring the bells, which bring death to any mortal who hears them. The nachzeher may also bring death to any unfortunate upon whom its shadow falls.

To destroy a nachzeher, one must place a coin inside the mouth and cut off its head with an ax. If there is a name in the corpse's clothing, it must be removed.

NELAPSI

NELAPSI These are Slovak Vampires that are known to rise from their graves and drink human blood, and they may massacre an entire village. Nelapsi may be detected when a corpse lacks rigor mortis, has open eyes, and has two curls in its hair. The skin of a nelapsi is white and unnaturally tough, and its clothes are indestructible.

Nelapsi are far stronger than mortals; they do not require food or drink, and they may penetrate holy places. They have two hearts, one to house their soul and one to house the soul of the demon who gives them their powers. They are strongest when in a holy place. If a nelapsi climbs a Church bell tower, it may slay all it sees with just a glance.

Fig. 15 A dreaded female nelapsi

They are nocturnal and sleep in their graves by day. A nelapsi may be prevented from rising at night by nailing its hair, limbs, and clothing to its coffin with blackthorn nails and then setting it on fire with holy oil.

The only true way to be sure that a nelapsi will not rise is to prevent their creation. To do this, a witch must be buried with holy symbols in the coffin and poppy seeds in her mouth. Poppies must also be planted on the grave. Some traditions maintain that the corpse must be destroyed by impaling the head or heart with a blackthorn or hawthorn stick. The family must go through ritual cleansing after the deed.

Nelapsi are justifiably considered the most dangerous of Vampires, and few will survive an encounter with one.

Fig. 16 Pijavica

OHYN This Polish Vampire is created when a child has teeth and a caul at birth. To prevent the child from becoming a Vampire, its teeth should be extracted, lest it die and awaken in the earth and consume its own flesh and bones.

PIJAVICA A Slovenian Vampire created as a result of having lived a particularly evil life. This miserable creature can be destroyed by decapitation, and its annihilation must be made complete by placing the head between its legs.

STRIGOII

The most common species of Vampire in Romania, strigoii are known as dead Vampires, while the living variety are called the moroii. The name strigoii comes from the ancient Greek word for screech owl, which also came to mean witch or demon.

The strigoii consort with the moroii, who join the ranks of their undead cousins upon death. There are many ways to become a strigoii, but death at the hands of a Vampire is the most common. Other causes include being the seventh son of a seventh son, being born with a caul, being cursed by a witch, or by dying unmarried with an unrequited love.

A corpse in the process of transforming into a strigoii has an open, staring left eye. The transformation may be prevented by stabbing a sickle through the heart of the corpse and sticking nine needles into the ground to pierce the creature as it rises.

Strigoiis usually have red hair, blue eyes, and two hearts. The second heart holds the strigoii's vitality. This is the heart that spurts blood if it is pierced by a stake.

A strigoii is believed to drink its victim's blood or feed upon the heart of the victim. Strigoii are also thought to be able to cause drought or floods.

In some tales a strigoii might prey on its former family, becoming invisible and behaving like a poltergeist, creating chaos and eating the family's food. Oftentimes members of its family or animals belonging to the household die after a visit by a strigoii.

Some believe that strigoii may shapeshift into a cat, dog, or sheep—sometimes they might even return as handsome young men. In the latter case, the death of a girl usually results.

To be rid of a strigoii, the corpse must be dug up and a stake driven into the heart. As an extra safeguard, the corpse may also be decapitated and the heart burned. People believe that if a strigoii is not destroyed within seven years of its burial, it

It is my fervent hope that I shall never find myself face to face with so devilish a creature as this!

C

Is my Transylvanian expedition entirely wise, I wonder...

may pass once again as a living human being. It then desists from preying on humans, but from Friday evening until Sunday morning it has to rest in a grave in the local cemetery. The children of such creatures are destined to become undead themselves.

"The child is cursed! The child is cursed, I tell you! The seventh son—and born with a caul! Terrible, treacherous child!" Anon.

Fig. 17 Strigoii

UBOUR

A rare Bulgarian Vampire; only the greater ubour is considered a true Vampire. This Vampire is created if the spirit refuses to leave a body after a violent death. Forty days after burial, the corpse digs itself out of its grave and starts to behave like a poltergeist in its former family home.

The eating habits of this Vampire are unusual, for it will consume normal food and does not seek out human blood unless it finds no other source of nourishment. The ubour is known to shapeshift into cat form.

ULSTREL

This Bulgarian Vampire preys on cattle. It is believed to be the spirit of a child born on a Saturday who dies without being baptized. Nine days after it is buried, it comes out of its grave to attack livestock and drink their blood. If an ulstrel attacks more than five cattle or sheep in any one night, the farmer must perforce hire a Vampirdzhija, or Vampire hunter, to destroy it.

Fig. 18 Upier

UPIER

A Polish Vampire that steals hearts. The upier sleeps much of the day, only rising between the hours of noon and midnight. This Vampire has a dangerous barbed tongue that it uses to consume vast amounts of blood. It has a legendary thirst and is reputed to sleep bathed in blood. It can be destroyed by a stake through the heart or decapitation.

Humans can become immune to attack from an upier by mixing Vampire blood with flour and consuming this baked blood bread. A corpse may be prevented from becoming a upier if it is buried facedown with a cross of willow under the armpits, chest, or chin.

The upyr is a Russian variant of this type of Vampire, which is considered to be extremely vicious. It has a tendency to attack children first, followed by their parents.

Fig. 19 Zmeu transforming
from flame to man

ŽMEU A Moldavian Vampire-like figure that takes the form of a flame, then enters the chamber where a young girl or a widow sleeps. Once inside, the flame becomes a man, who then abducts the woman.

A zmeu has many magical powers: He can fly and shapeshift into a variety of different creatures. He also has tremendous supernatural strength.

The Story of Asmund & Aswid

This is the tale of two Icelandic warriors in the old time. When Alf was king of Hethmark, he had a son named Asmund. At the same time the province of Wik was ruled by King Biorn, who had a son named Aswid. Both sons were brave and fearless warriors.

One day Asmund was out hunting but could find no quarry. A sudden mist came down over the land, and Asmund became separated from his fellow huntsmen. He was lost and wandered alone for a long time. He was parted from his horse, and his garments were reduced to tatters. He ate only berries and fungi and wandered aimlessly until he reached the place where King Biorn dwelled.

He was taken in and formed a friendship with Biorn's son, Aswid. The two men became inseparable and swore vows of brotherhood. Moreover, they swore that if either should die, the other would undertake to be buried alongside him so they could stay together forever.

Some time later Aswid became ill and died. He was buried with ceremony in a grave that was a cavern in the earth. His horse and dog were buried alongside him. And Asmund, true to his solemn oath of friendship, was bravely sealed alive in the grave with Aswid, together with food and other tributes to be used in the afterlife. The tomb was a deep vault. It had a huge stone rolled over the mouth, and a barrow of earth and stones piled over the top, as was the custom.

Some hundreds of years later, a band of Swedish soldiers came upon the burial barrow of Aswid and broke open the hill, thinking that there might be treasures buried within. They found a vault deeper than they had anticipated and dispatched a soldier to the depths, dangling him into the tomb in a basket affixed to the end of a strong rope.

What the soldiers drew up in the basket on the end of the rope was beyond any imagining. The figure of the old warrior Asmund emerged in place of their comrade. Asmund's face had a ghastly pallor and spurted fresh blood. The soldiers fell back in horror, and several fled the scene. To those brave enough to stay and question him, Asmund told this tale.

Aswid had risen from the dead at night as a Vampire and attacked all around him with demonic fury. First he devoured his own horse and his hound. He then launched a ferocious attack on his sworn blood brother. With his sword, Asmund had defended himself from Aswid. He had been fighting him ever since: His cheek had been slashed by Aswid's raking fingernails, and Aswid had almost wrenched off an ear.

All these years Asmund had fought off Aswid yet never finally defeated him until now. At last the Vampire had been impaled and his corpse decapitated. At the end of his tale, Asmund fell down dead at the feet of the soldiers. They hailed the bravery of this old warrior who had fought off the marauding Vampire for so many years and buried his body in the tomb with full military honors. The decapitated remains of Aswid they took up and burned, as tradition demands, and scattered his ashes to the four winds.

The Baby of Boureni

Once a young girl in the village of Boureni in Romania became pregnant. Her unborn baby was restless, and she promised it all manner of reward if it would lie peacefully. Eventually she promised to give it all the animals of her wealthy neighbors, and after this the child lay quietly.

When the girl's time came, she gave birth to a boy who was born with a caul. The baby died before it could be baptized and so was buried outside the consecrated cemetery, and it became a Vampire. Soon afterward, the sheep of the neighboring family began to die, one following another.

One night the shepherd saw the dead baby moving among the sheep in the form of a cloud. He hit the cloud with his crook and it became the head of a horse. Then the baby returned to its grave. The shepherd opened the grave and found that the baby had become a Vampire. With his sickle he cut the tiny corpse into pieces, cooked the pieces in wine, and reburied them. After that, no more sheep died.

The Countess of the Château de Deux-Forts

In the twelfth century a French countess lived in a castle called the Château de Deux-Forts. One night she found a strange brown spot upon her belly. She ordered her servants to scrub off the spot, first with cold then with hot water, but no matter how hard they scrubbed, the spot remained.

The next morning the spot seemed larger and the countess summoned her physician. He pronounced the countess to be suffering from leprosy. The countess threatened to have the physician skinned alive unless he found a cure.

The terrified physician told the countess that the only cure to be had was to bathe in fresh human blood. And from that day on, children began to disappear all through that region. Rumors were whispered about an evil ogre who ate children. Eventually the authorities investigated the disappearances and discovered the countess's bloody crimes.

The physician and all the servants were hanged for their part in the killings. The countess was sentenced to be quartered by four horses. A stone cross marks the scene of her execution. Its name is *La Croix de Male Mort*.

The Old Woman of Amarasesti

Many years ago, in the Romanian village of Amarasesti, a very old woman died. She was the mother of two sons. Some time later the children of both her sons began to weaken and die, one following another.

The sons became convinced that their mother had become a Vampire. So one night they opened her grave, removed the corpse, cut it in two, and buried both halves again. But the deaths continued. So they opened her grave a second time. To their horror they saw that the two halves had grown together again.

This time they took the corpse to a forest. There they removed her heart, from which fresh blood was flowing. They slashed the heart into four pieces and burned it. Then they cremated the corpse entirely. They carefully gathered the ashes and buried them in the grave. But they took home with them the ashes of the heart, mixed them with water, and gave them to the victims to drink. From that moment there were no more deaths.

PART TWO

HOW TO DEAL WITH
VAMPIRES

Ways in which *a* person *may* become *a* Vampire

Vampiric transformation at birth may happen in the following circumstances:

- BEING BORN AT CERTAIN TIMES of year, including at a new moon or on certain holy days
- BEING BORN WITH A RED CAUL, teeth, or an extra nipple
- BEING BORN WITH EXCESS HAIR, a red birthmark, or two hearts
- WHEN WEANED TOO EARLY or suckled after weaning
- THE SEVENTH SON OF A SEVENTH SON
- DYING BEFORE BEING BAPTIZED
- WHEN THE MOTHER DIDN'T EAT enough salt during pregnancy
- IF A VAMPIRE STARES at a pregnant woman

Vampiric transformation during life may come about if someone:

- COMMITS SUICIDE
- PRACTICES SORCERY OR WITCHCRAFT
- LIVES AN IMMORAL LIFE
- BECOMES A WEREWOLF
- DEVELOPS A TASTE FOR HUMAN BLOOD
- EATS SHEEP KILLED BY A VAMPIRE

Vampiric transformation at or after death may be caused by:

- Death at the hands of a VAMPIRE
- The WIND FROM THE RUSSIAN STEPPE blowing on a corpse
- A CAT JUMPING over the corpse
- A SHADOW FALLING on the corpse
- NOT BURYING a corpse, or administering improper rites
- Being VIOLENTLY KILLED
- An unrevenged MURDER
- A CANDLE being passed over a corpse
- A SLEEPWALKING brother (*this is very rare*)
- Death by DROWNING
- STEALING the ropes used to bury a corpse
- Being buried FACEUP in a grave (*parts of Romania*)

Methods *of* detecting *the* presence *of a* Vampire

Signs and portents at a grave or cemetery:

- Finger-size holes
- Disturbed earth or coffins
- Constant mist
- Moved or fallen tombstones
- Broken or fallen crosses
- Footprints from graves
- An absence of birdsong
- Dogs who refuse to enter
- Geese honking near a grave
- Horses shying from a grave
- Groaning heard from underground

Signs that might be noted on a corpse:

- Open eyes
- A ruddy complexion
- Fangs
- A bloated body
- New nails
- Long hair
- Flexible limbs (no *rigor mortis*)
- Lack of decomposition
- Blood around the mouth

Signs of attack in possible victims:

- Suffering sleeplessness or nightmares
- Bite marks on the neck
- Exhaustion, nervousness, and irritability
- Sleepwalking
- Difficulty in breathing
- Lack of appetite
- Weight loss
- An aversion to garlic

I fear for Mrs. Dobbs, a local socialite who exhibits many of these symptoms and habitually wears a scarf about her neck, or a high-necked dress. She has grown excessively thin of late.

Signs suggesting vampiric transformation:

- Fangs
- Red eyes
- Long nails
- Extreme pallor
- Reluctance to enter a house without invitation
- Hairy palms
- An aversion to bright lights
- Lack of appetite
- Not being seen during daylight hours
- No reflection in a mirror

Protection *from* Vampires

The following may afford a measure of protection from the threat of attack by Vampires.

Garlic

This is a most important element in Vampiric protection. Garlic flowers may be hung at entrances and throughout the house to prevent Vampires from entering. These may be dried or freshly gathered. Cloves from the bulb are also extremely efficacious, especially if the clove is slit and the juice therein rubbed upon the forehead and neck.

Holly

This is another useful plant in deterring Vampires from attempting entry. Boughs of holly may be hung around the house and nailed to doorways.

Fishing nets

It is a Greek custom to fasten fishing nets on doors and windows. It is well known that Vampires are obsessed with counting and will be distracted from entering by the task of counting all the knots in the nets.

Seeds

Several seeds prove useful in fighting off the attentions of a Vampire. Poppy seed administered to a Vampire or packed into a Vampire's grave will render him sleepy and disinclined to roam abroad in search of fresh blood. Other seeds believed to be efficacious include mustard and carrot seeds.

Grains

Like the seeds described above, oats and millet have a deterrent effect on Vampires.

Buy
Garlic
Nets
Poppy, mustard,
*   and carrot seeds*
Oats
Millet
Candles
Tar
Paintbrushes
Wooden stakes
Handbells

C

Holy water

This well-known Vampire deterrent needs no describing; the more recently blessed the better.

Juniper logs

A brightly burning fire of young juniper logs has great value in averting the would-be bloodsucker.

Bells

The constant ringing of bells is also reputed to keep Vampires at bay.

Candles

Filling the room with lit candles deters Vampires, who abhor light.

Incense

The scent of incense will quickly banish a Vampire.

Tar

Crosses of tar painted on doors and windows may prevent a Vampire from entering a house.

Other precautions

A household should also be equipped with sharp knives in order to stab a Vampire if necessary, mirrors (to detect the presence of a Vampire), and a supply of sturdy wooden stakes with which to stab a Vampire through the heart.

Methods *of* destroying *a* Vampire

Staking
The most certain way to dispatch a Vampire is to pound iron stakes through the coffin and into the ground while the Vampire is resting inside it.

Beheading
Decapitation is also certain to end the days of a Vampire.

Exposure to sunlight
Vampires are unable to bear sunlight falling directly upon them.

Cremation
A tried and tested method of exterminating a Vampire. The ashes should be scattered to the four winds or mixed with wine and given to any known victims, for their greater protection.

Piercing with sword
This should be done with one blow, directly through the heart with a silver-bladed sword.

Immersing in water
Vampires have a strong aversion to water, so a good remedy against Vampiricism is to bury the suspected coffin beneath running water.

Drenching in garlic and holy water
Both these are anathema to the Vampire.

Touching with crucifix
A crucifix will burn a Vampire at its touch, and he will never be seen again.

Trapping in grave
A branch of wild rose will trap a Vampire inside his grave. A hedge of thorny bushes, such as rose, hawthorn, bramble, and blackthorn, planted around the grave will also offer protection.

Extracting heart
Remove with a silver knife; burn the heart to ash.

Most helpful and instructive!

C

Less common methods

Recorded here are a few less frequently used methods of dispatching a Vampire, which may be of limited use.

~ Steal the Vampire's left sock (useful for only a few species). Fill the sock with soil, gravel, dirt, and rocks and throw it outside the village boundary, preferably into a river.
~ Boil the Vampire's heart in vinegar, oil, or wine.
~ Inject the Vampire with holy water.
~ Use animals such as cockerels, dogs, or white wolves.
~ Stab the Vampire with steel needles in the stomach. This causes them to dissolve.

Bottling a Vampire

This is the most powerful method of destroying a Vampire in Bulgaria. It may only be undertaken by a well-trained sorcerer as it is dangerous and requires both a powerful will and an experienced hand. The sorcerer carries a holy picture and a bottle and lies in wait for the undead. When the Vampire appears, the sorcerer ambushes it, driving it relentlessly across rooftops with no respite. When faced with the holy picture, the Vampire will be forced to enter the bottle, which may contain a favorite food as an additional lure (in Bulgaria this is manure).

Once the Vampire is in the bottle, a cork is put in, and the bottle is sealed with a small piece of the holy picture. The sorcerer screams in victory and hurls the bottle into a roaring flame, thus destroying the Vampire forever.

PART THREE

MONSTROUS CREATURES

BABA-YAGA

Baba-Yaga is a wild old woman of Slavic mythology. She is known to be a mistress of magic and a spirit of the forest who leads hosts of other spirits. Stories about Baba-Yaga can be found in Russian, Polish, Ukrainian, Croatian, Bosnian, Macedonian, and Serbian folklore.

In Russian tales Baba-Yaga is usually a fearsome witch with iron teeth who flies through the air on a broomstick made from silver birch. She resides in a log cabin that moves around on dancing chicken legs. Another name for her is Baba-Yaga Bony Legs because she is as thin as a skeleton, in spite of having a huge appetite. She is rumored to abduct and enslave children.

Her arrival brings a wild wind that makes the surrounding trees creak and moan while the leaves whirl around her. When she departs, she sweeps away all traces of herself with her broom.

Her hut spins around on its chicken legs and utters bloodcurdling screeches. It may be guarded by a fence made of bones and crowned with skulls whose blazing eye sockets illuminate the darkness.

Baba-Yaga rules the elements. Her faithful servants are three horsemen: the White Horseman, who represents day; the Red Horseman, who represents the sun; and the Black Horseman, who represents night. She has other servants in the form of three menacing pairs of hands, unattached to bodies, that appear out of thin air and do her bidding.

Some say that Baba-Yaga ages a year every time someone asks her a question. This is why she is often seen as a bad-tempered old witch. The only way she can be rejuvenated is by drinking tea brewed from blue roses. Those who bring her a gift of blue roses may be granted wishes as a reward.

It is thought that the phrase *"Turn your back to the forest, your front to me"* will gain the traveler admission to Baba-Yaga's hut.

Reminds me of my dear wife's great-aunt Agatha—she most certainly has the Baba-Yaga temper. . . .

C

Fig. 20 Baba-Yaga

Fig. 21 Banshee

BANSHEE The banshee (or bean-sidhe) is an Irish woman who appears in one of three guises: as a young woman, as a stately matron, or as a raddled old hag. She is most often seen wearing a hooded gray cloak or grave robe. In some manifestations a banshee has only one nostril on a sunken nose, a projecting front tooth, long, streaming hair, and hollow eye sockets. She has webbed feet because she lives by a river, where she is heard continuously wailing while washing the clothes of a man destined to die.

Irish legend says that banshees originally wailed only for five old-established families: the O'Neills, the O'Briens, the O'Connors, the O'Gradys, and the Kavanaghs. Intermarrriage has since extended this exclusive list.

In 1437, a banshee foretold the murder of King James I of Scotland. This is an example of the banshee in human form. There are records of human banshees appearing at the great houses of Ireland and the courts of Irish kings.

A banshee may also appear in a variety of other forms, such as a hooded crow, a stoat, a hare, or a weasel—all animals associated with witchcraft in Ireland.

Fig. 22 A banshee in crow form

One of my colleagues, Dr. Igor Rillerman, swears he saw such a creature when on a fishing trip to the United States. A very timid beast methinks. C

Fig. 23 Bigfoot, or sasquatch

BIGFOOT

The bigfoot, also known as *sasquatch*, derives from North American folklore. It inhabits remote forests in the northwest of the continent. The bigfoot may be large, hairy, and apelike in appearance, and some believe it to be related to the yeti of Tibet and Nepal.

The bigfoot is described as being between seven and ten feet tall, powerfully built, walking on two legs, and covered in dark red hair. Sightings in the last century include footprints in snow seen in 1811, measuring fourteen inches in length and eight inches in width; encounters reported by missionaries in 1834, 1840, and 1870; and reports from American Indians of giant creatures that stole their salmon. No harm to humans has been recorded.

BROWNIE

Brownies play a part in Scottish and English folklore and legends. This creature is known in Scandinavia as *tomte*, in Slavic tales as *domovoi*, and in German lore as *Heinzelmännchen*.

Brownies may invisibly reside in houses and help with household tasks in return for small gifts or food. All manor houses have a brownie, and a special seat by the fireside is reserved for him. If humans annoy or neglect this creature, it will become a troublesome nuisance.

"Not above forty or fifty years ago, every family had a brownie, or evil spirit, so called, which served them, to which they gave a sacrifice for his service; as when they churned their milk, they took a part thereof, and sprinkled every corner of the house with it, for the brownie's use."

John Brand, 1703

BUGBEAR

This creature of legend may also be known by the names hobgoblin and bugaboo. In England, during medieval times children were admonished not to stray far from home or misbehave for fear of the bugbear finding them.

In some folktales a bugbear is a goblin or specter that frightens or annoys people.

Female bugbears are believed to steal babies and raise them underground. Bugbear is also a term for a scarecrow.

Fig. 24 Bugbear

CATOBLEPAS
This four-legged, bull-like creature originates from Ethiopia. It has the body of a buffalo and a very large head like a hog's, which is so heavy that it always hangs down. Its eyes are downward-looking and bloodshot. Catoblepas is Greek for "that which looks downward." The beast has thick eyelids and a long, hanging mane. Its back is covered with protective scales.

A catoblepas can kill a man simply by looking at or breathing on him. It is known to eat poisonous plants and, when frightened, breathes noxious fumes from its mouth.

"*In other respects of moderate size and inactive with the rest of its limbs, only with a very heavy head which it carries with difficulty and is always hanging down to the ground. Otherwise it is deadly to humans, as all who see its eyes expire immediately.*" Pliny

CENTAUR
Half horse, half man, the centaur has its origins in Greek mythology. Centaurs have the head and upper body of a man, joined to the body and legs of a horse.

Legend has it that centaurs are descended from Centaurus, son of the god of music, Apollo. Centaurs are believed to be governed by the bestial part of their nature, and even a small quantity of wine may cause them to behave in a wild and violent manner.

Fig. 25 Sagittarius, a centaur

Fig. 26 Chimera

CHIMERA This beast is composed of the body parts of three different creatures: a lion, a goat, and a serpent. The chimera breathes fire. She is described in Greek mythology as the daughter of the giant Typhon and the serpent Echidna. Among her evil siblings are Cerberus, the hound of hell, and Hydra, the nine-headed water snake.

"She was of divine race, not of men, in the fore part a lion, in the hinder a serpent, and in the middle a goat, breathing forth in terrible manner the force of blazing fire." Homer, *The Iliad*

COCKATRICE OR BASILISK

The cockatrice is the most poisonous creature on earth. To see a cockatrice is to die. It resembles an enormous winged cockerel but has a serpent's tail. The coloring is yellow, with whitish markings on the crown of its head. When a cockatrice moves, half its body slides in a snakelike manner, but it carries the front half of its body upright and erect. Anything touched by its venomous breath dies—man, beast, or plant—so the cockatrice dwells in a desert of its own making.

Fig. 27 Cockatrice

Three things spell doom for a cockatrice: a weasel, a cock crowing, and the sight of its reflection in a mirror. The creature is believed to be hatched from an egg laid by a seven-year-old cock when the dog star Sirius is in the ascendant. The egg from which it hatches is spherical in shape and must be hatched by a toad. The hatching can take nine years.

Cockatrices are found particularly in Crete and Libya, where travelers always carry a cockerel for protection. During the Middle Ages, people believed that if a cockatrice was struck from horseback with a spear, poison would rise through the spear and kill both man and horse.

Fig. 28 Polyphemus
the Cyclops

CYCLOPS

A cyclops is a giant who has a single, round eye in the middle of his forehead and an evil disposition. Cyclops appear in many Greek myths and are associated with massive strength and bad temper.

DEMON Also known as daemon or dæmon, a demon is a malevolent supernatural being known in almost every culture of the world. Demons may be conjured up and controlled, though they often escape from the power of their conjurers.

The ancient Egyptians believed that demonic monsters might devour living souls while they traveled toward the afterlife. Greek demons appear in the works of Plato and other ancient authors. These are impure and wandering spirits who have been steeped in earthly vices and seek to ruin others.

"These spirits . . . are always mixing up falsehood with truth, for they are both deceived and they deceive; they disturb their life, they disquiet their slumbers; their spirits creeping also into their bodies secretly terrify their minds, distort their limbs, break their health. . . . The only remedy from them is when their own mischief ceases." Cyprian, Bishop of Carthage, third century A.D.

Some believe that demons can possess living creatures. Demonic possession may last for brief periods while the rest of the time the victim may appear normal. Only when a demon is in residence can its presence be detected.

Victims of demon possession exhibit four symptoms that may appear alone or together, for mere seconds at a time, and in varying degrees of intensity. These symptoms are violence, lust, greed, and an unnatural power of persuasion.

There are hundreds of named demons from many different cultures, ranging from *Abbadon* (one of the kings who rules the earth and will release hordes of demons at the end of time) to *Zepar* (a god of war who can change people's shapes, seduce women's hearts, or make women infertile).

Notorious demons include: LEVIATHAN, an enormous, invincible, armored whale that has seven heads, and BEELZEBUB, lord of the dung, who usually appears as a fly, a gigantic cow, or a male goat with a long tail. He has cavernous nostrils and two horns sprouting from his head.

I wonder whether I might enlist the aid of my old schoolfriend Peter, who has gone on to hold high office within the clergy. Perhaps he could provide some powerful evil-deflecting blessings for our hazardous enterprise...

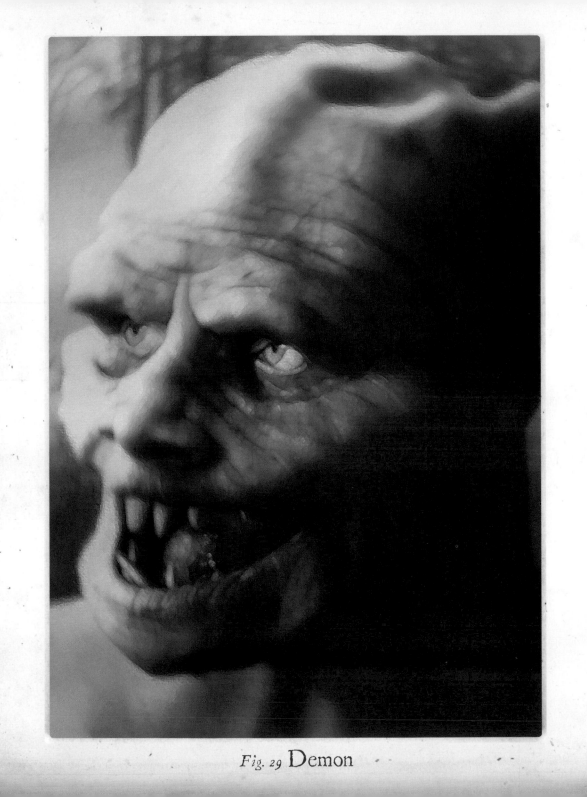

Fig. 29 Demon

DRAGON This supernatural beast has been known from the beginning of time by all peoples of the world as the guardian of treasure hordes.

A typical dragon has a huge, reptilelike body, plates, scales, and a row of spikes from head to tail, ending in a giant and deadly stinger. Witnesses describe its sharp fangs, round luminous eyes, spiked skull, forked tongue, vicious talons, and bats' wings. Dragons may be black, red (as the Welsh dragon), yellow, or white (as the Saxon beast).

Dragon's breath is believed to bring rain clouds, thunder, and lightning. From the frozen lands of Siberia come the fearful ice dragons, whose breath will freeze the blood of their victims. Africans say that dragons spring from the union of an eagle and a she-wolf: These dragons have three rows of teeth.

Dragons are believed to be the enemies of the sun and the moon and are often thought responsible for eclipses, which they cause when they are trying to swallow the sun. The Chinese dragon is believed to chase the sun in an attempt to bite it. A five-clawed dragon is the Chinese imperial symbol.

Dragons guard burial chambers, and dragons' teeth when planted will grow into an army of men. According to legend, Saint George (the patron saint of England) fought and killed a dragon in Libya to save the king's daughter, Sabra, from being sacrificed to it.

Norse mythology's most famous dragon is Fafnir, who was slain by Sigurd at the instigation of the dwarf Regin. Fafnir was Regin's brother, who had slain their father to steal his wealth, then shapeshifted into a dragon to protect his hoard. Sigurd slew Fafnir by hiding in a pit dug outside its lair and stabbing its vulnerable belly when the dragon passed over the pit. He then heard birds warning him that Regin planned to slay him and take the treasure, so he sliced off the dwarf's head and claimed the treasure as his own.

Fig. 31 Dwarf

Fig. 32 Ettin

DWARF

A dwarf is a short, stocky, hairy creature resembling a human but generally preferring to live underground or in remote mountains. Dwarfs are about the height of a three-year-old child, ugly and bigheaded.

These base creatures are associated with the earth, decay, and death. They are reputed to be able to see in darkness and to be skilled miners and smiths. Dwarfs have accumulated vast stores of gold, silver, and precious stones underground, and they spend much of their time crafting jewel-encrusted weapons and armor.

Dwarfs also have a reputation for being skilled warriors, although they run slowly and ride poorly. Some ascribe magical powers to the weapons that dwarfs have forged, and in many tales any hero posssessing a weapon created by dwarfs will find it cursed in some way so that it leads to death or murder.

ETTIN

This three-headed giant has its origins in Norse mythology and also appears in English folklore.

GHOUL

A ghoul is a cemetery-infesting demon, often a woman, who is half human and half fiend. She may have a gaunt face and bulging, yellowish eyes; her mouth is large and lined with rows of tiny, razor-sharp teeth. A ghoul's arms are long and thin and her hands clawed. The skin or hide is thick and fibrous and may be blue-gray in color.

Ghouls are not usually clothed, though they may wear the last vestiges of the garments they wore before they became ghouls. At night they prowl around graveyards and feed on the flesh of the newly dead. Their appetite is insatiable.

Ghouls appear in Arabian folklore as shapeshifting demons who live in deserts and other bleak, uninhabited places.

Fig. 33 Ghoul

They assume the form of a hyena and lure travelers to their deaths, devouring their bodies and drinking their warm blood.

When discovered, ghouls will growl or hiss to ward off intruders; they will only fight if cornered. They are difficult to defeat since they are impervious to pain, do not need air to breathe, and do not succumb to poison. Their powers of regeneration are astounding, so they can withstand gunshot or knife wounds.

Both sunlight and artifical light will repel a ghoul. Though neither will seriously harm them, light will reduce both their speed and strength, thus making them easier to destroy. Ghouls are highly susceptible to fire, concentrated acid, or electrocution. Decapitation has also proved an effective method of destruction.

This spells an end to my interest in unusual tombstones. I fear that I shall never be able to set foot inside a cemetery again without the hairs rising on the nape of my neck.

C

Fig. 34 Giant

GIANT
Mythological giants are creatures of enormous size who are the enemy of humans and do battle with the gods. They can be as tall as mountains and invincibly strong. Their shaggy hair droops from their heads and chins, and they have dragon scales on their feet. Giants are usually very stupid, greedy, and fond of human flesh.

Giants existed long before the gods and humans. When the gods first appeared, there followed a struggle between the two, which took its toll on the giants. When a giant was slain by a god, the god would create heaven and earth from the body of the giant.

GOBLIN
Goblins are a grotesque type of gnome. They may be playful, but they can be evil and perform harmful tricks on people. A goblin smile curdles the blood, and a goblin laugh sours milk and causes fruit to fall from trees. Goblins annoy humans in small ways, such as hiding objects, tipping over milk pails, and changing signposts.

Fig. 35 Goblin

Goblins originated in France and spread rapidly all over Europe. They have no homes and usually live in mossy clefts in rocks and the roots of ancient trees, although they never stay very long in the same place. Goblins sometimes move from place to place by hiding in carts of straw or in the holds of barges.

Their favorite food is duck or goose. Farmers in France nail silver coins to the doors of barns and henhouses to deter these troublesome creatures.

GOLEM

The golem is a manlike creature from Jewish folklore and legend that is usually created from a blob of clay and brought to life by mystical powers. In one case a golem was created from dead flesh. The most famous golem was created by Rabbi Yehuda Loew of Prague in the sixteenth century to defend the Jewish people there against accusations of murder. Legend has it that this golem is still hidden somewhere in the synagogue. Only the very righteous are able to bring a golem to life.

Fig. 36 Golem

GORGON

The gorgons are monstrous female creatures from Greek mythology. They are covered with impenetrable scales and have live snakes for hair, hands made of brass, sharp teeth, and a beard. Their appearance turns to stone anyone who looks upon them. Gorgons live near the ocean, guarding the entrance to the underworld. The stone head of a gorgon may be placed upon temples and graves to avert evil forces, and their symbol may be found upon the shields of soldiers. The Greek hero Perseus slew the terrible Medusa, one of three Gorgon sisters, by beheading her while she slept.

Fig. 37 Medusa the Gorgon

Note:

borrow pocket
trumpet from
Ludwig

C.

HARPY A winged female monster with long hair, brass claws, and a withered, hungry appearance. Everything a harpy touches is contaminated by a terrible stench. The only thing harpies fear is the sound of a brass trumpet.

HYDRA The hydra was a Greek monster with the body of a serpent and nine heads. One of these heads was impervious to any weapon, and if any of the other heads were severed, another grew in its place. This beast lived in the swamps near the ancient city of Lerna in Argolis. The stench from its breath was enough to kill man or beast. Every time it emerged from the swamp, it attacked and devoured herds of cattle and villagers.

Killing the hydra was the second task of the twelve legendary labors given to the Greek hero Hercules. He attacked the beast, slashing at each head with his sword, but he soon found that as one head was severed, another grew in its place. Hercules enlisted the help of his nephew Iolaus, who brought a flaming torch to cauterize the hydra's wounds and prevent the heads from growing again. Eventually Hercules had removed all but one of the heads. This last could not be harmed by a weapon, so Hercules crushed it with a blow from his club, then tore it from the hydra's body with his bare hands, and buried it deep in the ground, placing a huge boulder on top. Then Hercules dipped the tips of his arrows in the hydra's poisonous blood, making them deadly.

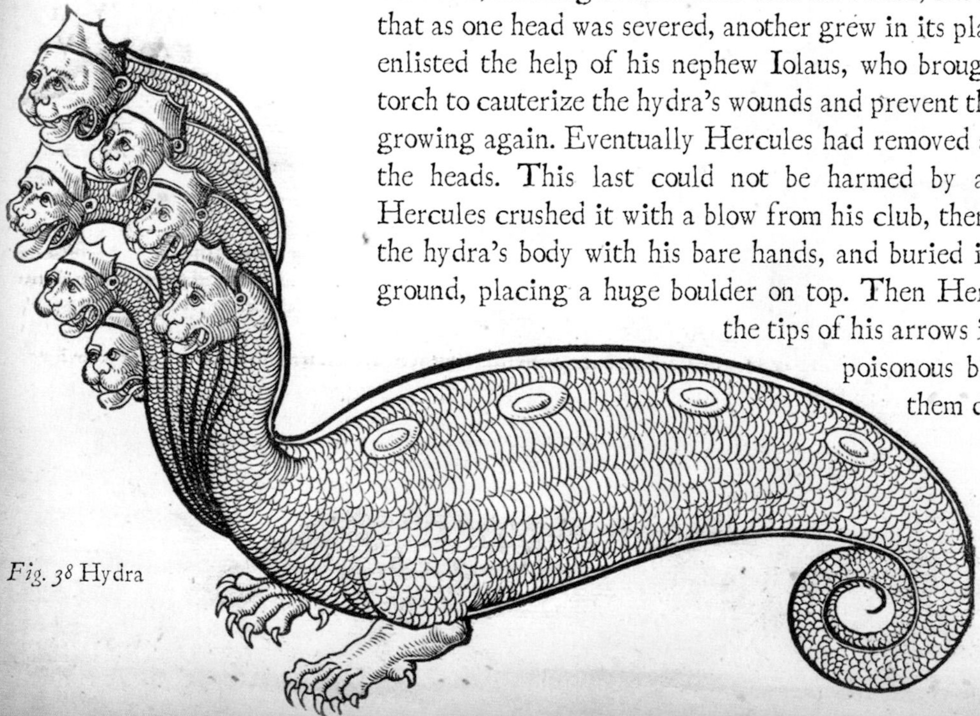

Fig. 38 Hydra

Fig. 39 Imp troubling
an innocent man

IMP Imps are mischievous and lively supernatural beings of small stature. They are dark and shadowy creatures that are frequently destructive but do not wreak the havoc caused by a gremlin or poltergeist. Imps shapeshift into the shadow forms of either a weasel or a spider, and they slink between pools of shadow. Their misdemeanors usually involve moving or hiding small objects or causing humans to trip or stub their toes. Some believe that imps are lonely creatures who travel in pairs or large groups. Imps were familiar spirits that served witches in the Middle Ages. They were kept inside artifacts, such as gemstones or phials, and summoned when needed.

Sometimes I think our household harbors an imp! No helpful advice about ridding us of it here, alas.

C

KELPIE

This shapeshifting creature of Celtic legend is reputed to be in league with the devil. A kelpie may appear as a gray or black horse with hooves that point backward. It can shapeshift at will, transforming into a beautiful white horse. If a

man mounts a kelpie, it will immediately gallop into water and drown him. The kelpie then eats the flesh of the drowned rider. Kelpies may also be part horse and part bull, with two sharp horns.

A kelpie may shapeshift into a handsome young man. The only clue to his identity is the waterweed tangled in his wet hair. If a young woman succumbs to his charm, she is certain to end her days in a watery grave.

Fig. 40 Kelpie, *or* Brook Horse

The stolen bridle of a kelpie may be used to work magic. Also, if a man can harness a kelpie with the bridle of an ordinary horse, he may control the kelpie.

KRAKEN

This giant, mythical sea monster is feared by sailors because of its astounding size and strength. The kraken may be up to a mile and a half long and have horns like masts. It spends most of its time lying on the seabed.

When the kraken surfaces, sailors may mistake it for a series of islands and land upon it. The creature then submerges and drowns them. The kraken's tentacles are strong enough to seize and wreck a warship. Its descent to the seafloor creates a fearsome whirlpool that sucks in and destroys ships for miles around.

Fig. 41 Kraken

Fig. 42 Leprechaun

LEPRECHAUN   These very small sprites live in farmhouses or cellars. They sometimes perform small tasks for humans. Leprechauns are called fairy cobblers, for they make shoes for elves (but always one shoe, and never a pair). They are merry creatures dressed in green, with a red cap, leather apron, and buckled shoes. When they finish their work, leprechauns organize wild feasts. Most leprechauns possess a treasure (often a pot of gold) that a human may take if he can capture the Leprechaun, but this is an extremely difficult task.

MANTICORE   This monstrous creature lives in the forests of Indonesia, Malaysia, and India. A manticore has a red body like a lion's, with a tail covered in poisoned spines and ending in a scorpion's stinger. Its head takes a human form, and in its mouth are three rows of razor-sharp teeth.

The manticore stalks humans. It moves very swiftly and can make powerful leaps. When it finds a victim, it fires off a volley of poisoned spines that bring instant death. It then consumes the victim entirely, from his blood and bones to his clothing, and also devours any possessions. The manticore's roar is like the sound of pipes and a trumpet together.

Fig. 43 Manticore

MINOTAUR

This Cretan monster was created because of Minos of Crete, who fought his brothers for the right to be king. He prayed to the god Poseidon to send him a snow-white bull, as a sign of his approval. In return, he promised to sacrifice the bull. A handsome white bull rose from the sea in response, but Minos did not keep his part of the bargain. He kept the handsome bull, sacrificing another bull in his place.

Fig. 44 The Minotaur

In revenge, Poseidon made Minos's wife fall in love with the bull. Together they produced a monster called the minotaur. This creature had the head and tail of a bull and the body of a man. It caused such terror and destruction on Crete that Minos built an intricate labyrinth in which he confined the beast. Every year thereafter for nine years, seven young men and seven maidens from Athens were sacrificed to the minotaur.

The Greek hero Theseus wanted to end the sacrifices and went to Crete as one of the victims. On his arrival, he met Ariadne, the daughter of Minos, who fell in love with him. She promised to help him escape from the maze if he agreed to marry her. When Theseus agreed, she gave him a ball of thread, the end of which he fastened near the entrance of the maze. He made his way through the maze, unwinding the thread, and stumbled upon the sleeping minotaur. He killed the beast and led the other sacrificial victims back to the entrance by following the thread, and they made their escape.

Fig. 45 Mummy

MUMMY
A mummy is a corpse whose skin and flesh have been preserved. Many mummies were embalmed, such as those made by the ancient Egyptians. They believed that the body should be preserved for the afterlife, so they opened the abdomen of a corpse and removed the organs. The empty body was then preserved in salts, covered with strips of white linen, and wrapped in canvas. Masks were made to protect the mummy and to allow the spirits to recognize the mummies when they returned to the tomb.

A number of other civilizations practiced the art of mummification, including the Aztecs and Incas. Some mummies may be naturally preserved by extreme cold or extreme dryness.

NIX
This Scandinavian water spirit plays enchanting songs on the violin and lures women and children to drown in lakes or streams. The nix is an adept shapeshifter and can sometimes be seen as a man playing the violin in streams and waterfalls but can also appear as a floating object or even an animal such as a river horse. Others describe the male as old and dwarfish but sometimes appearing as a golden-haired boy with slit ears and cloven feet, playing enchantingly on the harp.

The music of the nix is most dangerous to women and children, especially pregnant women and unbaptized children.

Fig. 46 Nix

He is believed to be most active during Midsummer's Night, on Christmas Eve, and on Thursdays. The nix may also be seen as an omen for drowning accidents; he may scream at a particular spot in a lake or river in which someone later drowns.

The rarer female nix is beautiful and sometimes has a fishtail. She lures men to drown. A nix may also appear as a horse who tempts a human to mount, then drowns him or her by dashing into water.

OGRE

Ogres are fierce, malign creatures who live on human flesh. They are larger and broader than a man but shorter than a giant. Ogres have a large, ugly head—often either bald or abundantly hairy—and a huge belly.

Some ogres may be shy and cowardly, with low intelligence, so humans may defeat them with ease. Many believe that ogres can shapeshift at will and that they live underground. The female ogress is associated with water and is believed to be less malicious than her male counterpart.

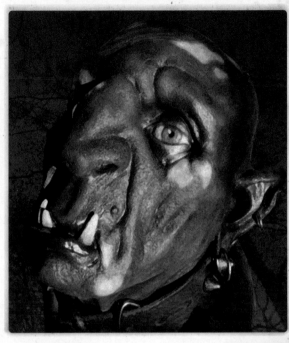

Fig. 47 Ogre

PHOENIX

The phoenix is a sacred bird with exquisite red and gold plumage that first appears in the myths of ancient Egypt. It is believed to be extremely long lived, surviving for hundreds, even thousands of years. At the end of its life, a phoenix builds a nest of twigs and sets it alight. Both bird and nest are consumed by the conflagration, and a new, young phoenix rises from the ashes. The bird is reputed to regenerate if injured, and its tears may heal wounds. The Chinese revere the phoenix as the leader of all birds and respect it almost as much as the dragon.

Fig. 48 The Phoenix

I have seen other pictures of such creatures. They appear laughable at first, but the stories surrounding these monsters are far from funny!

Fig. 49 Sea Troll

TROLL

TROLL The troll is a supernatural creature living mainly in the mountains and forests of Scandinavia. The rare sea troll is confined to remote fjords and coastal regions. Trolls can appear human but may have a hidden tail. They may be as huge as a giant or as small as a dwarf. Many live to be hundreds of years old. A male troll may have a large, crooked nose, quantities of coarse hair, and a bushy tail. He is immensely strong and may be horribly ugly; some have more than one head. The female troll often appears as lovely and may only be detected by the tail beneath her skirt.

Fig. 50 Male Troll

Trolls are shapeshifters, appearing as cats, dogs, or snakes—even taking on the shape of a fallen tree or a ball of yarn. Most of the time they remain invisible, though travelers may hear them talking or smell their freshly baked bread deep in a forest. They live underground beneath large boulders, where they hoard gold.

Fig. 51 Giant Troll

Trolls may be hostile to humans. They are thieves and visit feasts to eat all the food or spoil the beer. Many create mirages, such as imaginary fires. They also spirit people away. These stolen people are called *bergtagna* (meaning "taken to the mountain"), and if they return to their homes they are grievously changed in their minds. Beware, for trolls will steal cattle or even newborn babies, leaving their offspring in return. Night is when trolls are active; they disappear at sunrise. Some may turn to stone when exposed to sunlight.

Do not make an enemy of a troll. To keep on good terms with a troll, a traveler should put beer and porridge beside a bog or a wood. If pleased, a troll may help a human, but if a human gives a troll a possession, the troll will gain mastery over him.

Fig. 52 Werewolf

WEREWOLF

A werewolf is a man who is transformed into a wolf under the influence of a full moon. The ability of a werewolf to shapeshift may be voluntary or involuntary, hereditary or acquired. Werewolves are only active at night, when they devour children and corpses.

Werewolves have enormous strength and may be as strong as a dozen men. They have excellent nocturnal vision and a highly developed sense of smell. Werewolves are immune from aging and from most physical diseases because their body tissues constantly regenerate. This means that a werewolf may be virtually immortal. However, werewolves must return to human form and follow the same rules as ordinary humans.

Fig. 53 The scourge of
the werewolf

There are many ways of becoming a werewolf. The simplest is to remove clothing and don a belt made of wolfskin. A whole wolfskin may also be worn. Drinking water from the footprint of a werewolf or from certain enchanted streams also results in transformation. A child born on December 24 may become a werewolf. It is also said that the seventh son of a seventh son will become one. The most common cause of transformation is being bitten by a werewolf.

Various methods exist for removing the beast-shape. These include kneeling in one spot for a hundred years, being saluted with the sign of the cross or addressed three times by name, being given three blows on the forehead with a knife, or having at least three drops of blood drawn. Many believe that throwing an iron object over or at a werewolf will make it reveal its human form.

According to legend, werewolves may be killed by silver weapons. When a werewolf dies, he returns to his human form.

Gustav and I must arm ourselves well against these loathsome beasts. My great-grandfather's ceremonial silver dagger may find new purpose before the year is out. Sometimes I suffer the gravest doubts about the outcome of our journey east. . . .

C

WIGHT Wights are supernatural beings that originate in Norse mythology. There are both land-wights and sea-wights. More common are the land-wights, which are similar in appearance to humans, though smaller in stature. They may be strikingly beautiful and always wear gray garments.

Wights dwell underground. Road builders may divert the path of the road to avoid the home of a wight. Country folk warn the local wight if they are about pour hot water on the ground, to avoid retribution such as killed livestock, disease, or accidents. Wights have tiny livestock of their own, including cattle that are reported to produce vast quantities of milk. They may become invisible and also shapeshift into animals, especially toads. Children may see wights more often than adults.

The lesser known sea-wight is respected by sailors. When Norse seafarers approached land, they would remove the carved dragons from the bows of their longships to avoid frightening or insulting these creatures.

Fig. 54 Yeti

YETI Yeti means "magical creature," and the Nepalese call it a *rakshasa*, which is Sanskrit for demon. Sightings in the glaciers and crevasses of the Himalayas have been recorded since 1832. According to legend, there are three species of yeti: the Rimi, the Nyalmot, and the Raksi-Bombo. They vary in size but generally resemble each other.

A yeti has reddish hair and smells very strongly. It has enormous strength and may throw large boulders as though they were mere pebbles. The creature may howl or whistle and has been heard roaring like a lion. It is rumored to be fond of strong alcoholic drinks. Some believe the yeti is a descendant of a race of giant apes who retreated into the Himalayas half a million years ago.

Fig. 55 Zombie

ZOMBIE
A zombie is a dead person whose body is brought back to life by a curse. In Afro-Caribbean voodoo the zombie serves a sorcerer as a slave. The zombie's soul may have left the body through death rituals, but it may also have been removed from a living body by the power of the sorcerer.

Zombies never sleep and never become tired. They do not feel pain and do not need air to breathe. Drugs and poisons have no effect on them. If a zombie loses a limb, it will not die, and if it is decapitated, the head will continue to exist without the body. Some zombies crave human flesh and devour it at every opportunity.

A person bitten by a zombie will sicken and die in days. There is no known cure, and the victim also turns into a zombie.

INDEX